W9-CCE-634

The Royal Tea Party

This book belongs to:

Princess _____

gigi

God's Little Princess®

The Royal Tea Party

By Sheila Walsh

Illustrated by Meredith Johnson

THOMAS NELSON
Since 1798

NASHVILLE   DALLAS   MEXICO CITY   RIO DE JANEIRO   BEIJING

GIGI, *GOD'S LITTLE PRINCESS*®: THE ROYAL TEA PARTY
Text © 2006 by Sheila Walsh
Illustrations © 2006 by Thomas Nelson, Inc.

All rights reserved. No portion of this book may be reproduced, stored in a retrieval system, or transmitted in any form or by any means—electronic, mechanical, photocopy, recording, scanning, or other— except for quotations in critical reviews or articles, without the prior written permission of the publisher.

God's Little Princess® is a trademark of Sheila Walsh, Inc. Used by permission. All rights reserved.

Published in Nashville, Tennessee, by Thomas Nelson. Thomas Nelson is a trademark of Thomas Nelson, Inc.

Thomas Nelson, Inc., books may be purchased in bulk for educational, business, fund-raising, or sales promotional use. For information, please e-mail SpecialMarkets@ThomasNelson.com.

Scripture taken from THE MESSAGE. Copyright © 1993, 1994, 1995, 1996, 2000, 2001, 2002. Used by permission.

Scriptures identified (ICB) are from the *Holy Bible, International Children's Bible*® (ICB). Copyright © 1986, 1988, 1999 by Thomas Nelson, Inc.

ISBN 13: 978-1-4003-0800-2 (S-2008)

Library of Congress Cataloging-in-Publication Data
Walsh, Sheila, 1956 –
    The royal tea party / by Sheila Walsh ; illustrated by Meredith Johnson.
    p. cm.
  "Gigi, God's little princess."
  Summary: Gigi tells her friend Frances that they are both "God's little princesses."
  ISBN 1-4003-0800-3 (hardcover)
  [1. Christian life—Fiction. 2. Friendship—Fiction.] I. Johnson, Meredith, ill. II. Title.
  PZ7.W16894Per 2006
  [E]—dc22
                                2005023655

Printed in China
08 09 10 11 12 RRD 11 10 9 8

This book is
dedicated to all of
God's Little Princesses.
Being loving and kind
is more important than
getting everything
right!

Gigi had big news.

She sat on the bed with her cat discussing her problem.
"Lord Fluffy, it is my royal duty as princess to tell Frances the good news," she said. "How shall I make my announcement?"

Lord Fluffy seemed more concerned with Gigi's bunny slippers than with her exciting news.

"Certainly not!" she cried indignantly. "One does not pounce on a princess with this kind of news. It has to be delivered . . . very carefully. I am sure Frances will faint this time."

"Daddy, if you had to deliver wonderful but very important news and there wasn't a moment to spare, how would you do it?" Gigi asked the next morning at breakfast.

"I think I would pick up the phone, princess, if the news was urgent," he said.

"Hmm, I was trying to find something more . . . royal," Gigi said.

Let the teaching of Christ live in you richly. Use all wisdom to teach and strengthen each other. . . .

Colossians 3:16 (ICB)

Gigi lay on her bed and tried to think of ways a princess could make a royal announcement. "I've got it! I could have a band. There must be a procession!"

She picked up her pink telephone and began to dial.

"Maggie, this is Gigi," she said. "I need you to play for a royal announcement tomorrow. How would you like to be a part of Gigi's Pink Parade Players?"

"Sorry, Gigi, but I have dance class tomorrow," her friend replied.

"But this is important!" Gigi said. "And one would consider it an honor just to be asked!"

"Sorry," Maggie replied. "But if you want, you can borrow my flute."

"Do you think I could learn to play in one night?" Gigi asked.

"Well, perhaps not."

Gigi tried all her friends, but it was no use. The answer was always the same. "Sorry, but . . .

"My dog ate my drum!"

"I broke my pinkie finger."

"My brother sat on my trumpet."

"My lizard is loose!"

Suddenly it came to her. "I shall simply have to hire a band."
Gigi took her pink piggy bank off the shelf and emptied out
the contents.

"I don't think this will be enough," she said. "I think I would
need at least five dollars."

"I know!" Gigi said jumping up and down on her bed. "I could make my announcement on TV."

Gigi imagined herself standing in front of the camera:
"Hello, America, this is Princess Gigi interrupting your regularly scheduled program with an important announcement! Frances is God's little princess too!"

"Too dangerous," Gigi decided, "Frances would definitely faint."

"A small plane—that's what we need, Lord Fluffy! We could fly low over Frances's house with a humongous sign."

"No, too predictable," she said.

"Now I've really got it!" she cried so loudly that Lord Fluffy shot up in the air. "We will have a royal tea party. That is the proper way."

"And Frances will love it."

Gigi ran downstairs to ask Mommy.

"Mommy, may I invite Frances for a royal tea party tomorrow?"

"I think that would be lovely," her mommy replied. "Is it a special occasion?"

"The most special of all," Gigi said. "Tomorrow I will tell Frances that she is a princess too. What joy!"

Gigi started preparing right away. "Mommy, do you know where the balloons are?" she asked.

"They're in a big box in the playroom, Gigi," Mommy said. "How many do you need?"

"I need a lot . . . and I can only use pink ones for the royal cat-drawn carriage," Gigi replied.

"What's the cat-drawn carriage for?" Mommy asked.

"I feel that I should deliver the invitation in person," Gigi replied.

Gigi sat on the floor and blew—

and blew   and blew   and blew.

Soon Gigi had six pink balloons but was feeling . . . not-so-in-the-pink.

Gigi and Lord Fluffy set off as Mommy watched from the porch. "Oh! Mommy, will you call Frances and ask her to look out of her window?" Gigi asked.

"Tail up, Lord Fluffy! You should be thrilled to be part of the royal announcement parade."

As they approached Frances's house, Lord Fluffy jumped out and ran away, balloons dragging. Gigi was horrified.

She looked up at Frances's bedroom window. "I'm going home! *Everything* has gone wrong!"

"This has been one of the worst days in my whole life!" Gigi announced to Mommy. "I quit!" she added. "Frances will just have to live in ignorance of the extremely large hugeness of what I had to share."

"Do you think Frances would quit on you, Gigi?" Mommy asked gently. "Or do you think that God would quit on us if we didn't understand at first how much He loves us?"

"No, Mommy, I'm sure God would never quit on His little princesses."

When Gigi came downstairs in her p.j.'s, Daddy was laughing.

"What's so funny, Daddy?" she asked.

"I just got off the phone with Frances's father. He wants to know if she can stop looking out of the window now!"

"She was still looking?" Gigi asked with a smile.
"She really is a very good friend! Perhaps I should
just call her and invite her to the tea party after all."

The next day, the two friends sat out in the yard talking.
Soon Mommy brought out the tea tray.

"Thank you, Mommy," Gigi said.

"Yes, thank you," Frances added. "Gigi, what were you going
to show me yesterday?"

"I looked out of the window for hours, but the only thing I saw was your cat running through the yard with balloons!"

Gigi sighed with embarrassment. "Let's just ask the blessing."

"Dear God, thank You for my friend Frances and for the wonderful news that I have been trying to tell her for days . . . that she is Your daughter and God's little princess just like me, but it's been very hard and things kept going wrong and I almost quit, but Frances didn't quit on me and You don't quit on us, so I am here once more to announce to Frances that she is Your princess too, and I'm going to let her use the royal cup so now she knows and . . . and . . . and . . . Amen!"

Before the world was made, God decided to make us his own children through Jesus Christ.

Ephesians 1:5 (ICB)

Gigi opened her eyes and smiled. Things had gone even better than expected. As she moved the royal cup to Frances's side of the table, she gazed down at her best friend lying flat on the grass.

Frances had fainted!

Gigi knelt beside her dazed friend and said, "This is the best day of our lives, Frances. We are both God's little princesses!"

God chose you out of all the people on Earth
as his cherished personal treasure.

Deuteronomy 14:2